Alex Clark

How to quit wishing you were someone else

This book was professionally typeset on Reedsy
Find out more at reedsy.com

Contents

1.

2.

3.

4.

5.

6.

7.

8.

9.

I

Be the best you can to your self

1

Ways to stop wishing you were someone else

Normally Some people are afraid of maintaining their anonymity. Everyone aspires to be somebody and have their name publicly recognized. They have a strange sense that they must be exceptional. Sometimes being ordinary is amazing in the world of extraordinary people. People are willing to give up their peace, harmony, and pleasure in the quest for that which makes them extraordinary. A few people do rise beyond the norm and may briefly become renowned. But consider the cost that must be borne. People in the East are aware of their inherent extraordinary. It is sufficient to feel alive and a part of existence.

People must always stay one step ahead of everyone else because they want to be extraordinary. If everyone in the world is competing with one another to be better than them, nothing but a wild rush can result. the crazed pursuit of knowledge, technology, trivia, power, and so forth. Our relationships with other people suffer the most because this is a race, and second place is never good enough in a race. Therefore, before discussing ourselves or others, we should consider how we wish to relate to them. We cannot be competitive and aggressive if we wish to be cordial and helpful and combative.

It is important to first decide the type of relationship we want to have with those around us before considering the traits we must acquire to make that relationship possible. We must leave the race and the rivalry behind. Prior to deciding how to proceed, we must first decide on the relationship. We frequently operate in the opposite manner. We don't have time to accommodate other people into our life in any other way except on our own terms since we are constantly competing and running. Others are then attempting to integrate us into their life according to their terms.

What is wrong with being ordinary, you could ask? Don't just be average; compete and be the greatest is the Western style of thinking, which encompasses everything. Being commonplace makes Easterners happy since it is extraordinary in and of itself. The Eastern mind accepts reality as it is and recognizes beauty via comprehension, as opposed to striving and reaching for the impossibly impossible.

Just keep it in mind.

You are special. There is nobody else like you in the entire universe. Nobody who is exactly like you has ever been born or will ever be born. Imagine being truly unique and having the opportunity to perform as yourself on the stage of life. You don't need to act artificially or forcefully, pretend to be someone else, or do anything else. Things are already happening for you, so there's no need to wait for them to. Nothing can make you any better than you already are, either just be proud of your self.

It might also be beneficial to sit down and consider whether the person you're aspiring to be like is doomed to pass away over the next five years. This can help you value yourself highly and concentrate on your own goals rather than those of others.

comprehending that you wouldn't necessarily be happy even if you were someone else. You can modify yourself if you feel like you need to, but doing so won't cause you to change who you are; rather, it will make you a better version of who you already are.

There is no such thing as absolute happiness, but sometimes it seems like other people are happier and more successful than we are. They also appear to have the things we want and need, but we never stop to consider what they might be lacking. All we can do is set goals for our lives, pursue those goals, and transform into the people and experiences we desire .

I had exactly the same thing. I tried to piece together a mask of many looks and personalities that belonged to people or characters that I adored because I wanted to be other people. Predictably, the outcome was not favorable.

But I discovered that my thoughts and fantasies were the true source of my yearning to be someone else. I made the decision to attempt thought control as a result. I discovered that it's essentially impossible, but you can try the following:

When I first started meditating, I found that I could control my awareness more precisely. I also discovered that by focusing on my breathing, I could bring my awareness back to my body and away from my fantasies. You should give it a try since it helps you become more grounded in who you are and teaches you a lot about yourself in ways that language just cannot. There are many gurus who are eager to take your money and lead you through this very enigmatic inner journey. You can do it yourself if you're brave and with this you can focus more on your self and grow bigger.

Hence Because you think your own self is unimportant or inadequate, you may have a tendency to wish to be someone else.

Start by identifying your positive traits and strong points and concentrating on those. List everything. Even if you are miserable right now, you can still make this list.

Love yourself for who you are, second. and "desire" to develop oneself more.

Third, as you proceed along this route, you begin to develop into a distinctive individual whom you respect. Then repeat step 1 by going back.

Watch your development. You'll adore it.

Being authentic involves maintaining your beliefs and ideals and not letting them change because of the people you are with. Therefore, you are being yourself when your beliefs, words, and actions are in harmony.

To avoid feeling pressured into purchasing a drink, merely declare, "I don't drink," when out to lunch with a group of colleagues who drink. You are now expressing who you are, just be real in life and see your leaving more happy in life

2

Why is it so tough to love oneself?

I can relate to you because we were essentially in the same position. So, here's why it's so challenging to love oneself:

* We often hear statements like "You are valuable," "Each soul has incalculable worth," and "We are all attractive, talented, and great in our own ways," and we sometimes even begin to believe them. Then we venture out into the harsh world where people assess us, where we are judged, and where we eventually learn to judge ourselves. Our sense of self-worth has abruptly disappeared. This self-doubt system frequently includes our own parents or family.

* We frequently focus more on unpleasant than pleasant experiences. We'll never forget the moment our teacher called us dumb or the cute high school boy called us ugly, but we dismiss the numerous compliments on our intelligence and beauty from those who know and love us. We choose to cling to the negatives rather than acknowledge all the good proof of our worth and beauty.

*

We lack self-confidence. We ignore the internal whispers of our value in favor of the overwhelming messages from outside that cast doubt on us. Then we start seeking for ways to increase our "esteem" in the world, whether it be by outperforming others, finding the ideal companion, or developing into a perfectionist in order to feel deserving of love. But since each of these routes to "self-esteem" is based on a system of self-doubt, they will all ultimately fail.

Suggestions

1 2 Recall that you are evaluating yourself against perception. When we compare ourselves to others, whether it be in terms of public perception, appearance, friendships, a career, or a particular achievement, we are only doing so in terms of how we see them. We are not that person, and we will never know who they truly are. It's acceptable to respect traits like work ethic, style, and humor, but remember that these qualities are only a small part of a person. Moreover, you can never be sure.

2, The boasting should be avoided. I had a hard time doing this. I still occasionally feel bitter or envious of other people's achievements. However, a wise friend once stated that everyone in our community was successful enough. It can be quite challenging to celebrate another person's accomplishments when you so much want your own. However, you don't really want their success; instead, decide what your own success should be, regardless of others.

3 past the figures. Link bait, Instagram, and Facebook all contribute to the exacerbation of these emotions of inadequacy brought on by comparison to others. It could seem like everyone is boasting about something except for you. Though quantifiable metrics like Instagram followers or click through are just that—numbers—numbers, they are nonetheless. There are methods to systematically increase followers and likes.

4 You are the sole individual. Although it may sound corny, there is one of you. Your experiences and worldview are completely unique, just like you. You are valuable and fairly wonderful because of it. Because you cannot be anyone else, be the finest version of yourself that you are capable of becoming. There will always be someone taller, more intelligent, more attractive, or more wealthy than you. It is both physically impossible and a losing endeavor to.

Believe what you see because even if you change, you'll be a new person, and who knows? Maybe people will like you that way! And is the only thing you desire being acknowledged, appreciated, and pampered? In your twenties, you'll discover that these are pointless. Realize you have what they lack rather than believing you lack what they possess.

3

25 Easy Ways To Get People To Like You

You've probably encountered people in your life who you found more endearing than the majority of those you've met.

Maybe they were great at making people laugh, or maybe they were just really good at admitting their flaws.

You can exhibit particular personality qualities to endear people to you wherever you are—at work, a party, or simply out in public.

I used to spend a lot of time trying to impress people when I was younger. But as I got older, I realized that, more often than not, if you just have fun, people will love being around you too.

These psychological techniques are effective strategies to make friends, acquire respect, get people talking to you, and perhaps even attract someone's attention and make them like you back. Here are a few strategies you can use to win people over either immediately or gradually.

The following advice could make you everyone's favorite

1. Ask the things you want to know.

People appreciate it when others are interested in their knowledge or life experiences.

People like giving answers when they're asked questions to help them understand something.

This is a quick approach to get someone to talk to you well. I was one of those kids who didn't know what to say to people when we were younger.

For instance, most of the time when I was talking to girls on the phone, I had no idea what questions to ask.

But as time went on, I mastered the art of posing real inquiries. Personally, I find it annoying when people inquire merely for the sake of inquiry. The dialogue becomes artificial and forced as a result.

Everyone is interested in learning something about someone. When you can get the answers to the questions you're actually curious about, you'll be able to appreciate the conversation much more.

Additionally, the responses can lead to further inquiries and more in-depth discussion, which would increase the person or individuals you are with real admiration for you.

2. Sometimes, talk more

Some individuals excel at the art of conversation. They are popular because they talk nonstop. Try being more vocal about your feelings and thoughts.

Being more of an introvert myself, I realize not everyone finds it to be the easiest. But with enough experience, you can feel a little more at ease speaking up when you want to.

3.

3 Give others your time in a selfless manner

People appreciate those who are willing to lend a helping hand without expecting anything in return.

It's possible that you've had someone assist you in understanding or doing particular responsibilities at work without expecting anything in return. My guess is that you were grateful to them for it.

One thing to bear in mind when giving assistance to others is to always be sincere.

4. Be modest

Nobody enjoys an arrogant expert. People respect those who have the humility to admit that occasionally they might need our assistance or wisdom. Most people do not find it endearing when someone acts as though they are the wisest or know everything.

5 Be a good listener.

While talking more can increase like ability, listening well is equally important. Spend some time letting people respond to you with whatever is on their mind.

Try to learn something new about the person you're speaking to it can really help.

6 Make others laugh

Almost everyone enjoys being around people who can make them and others laugh. It's not necessary to be a comic,Finding the funny things is all that is required. Most people will likely grin at you, if not laugh.

7 Lessen your aggression

Despite the fact that we all have our own likes and tastes, people tend to favor those who are adaptable. Additionally, they enjoy those who don't impose their preferences on them.

Most people will respect you if you can easily adapt to changing circumstances.

8 Relax

Yes, life can be serious at times, and we occasionally need to be as well. However, try not to constantly bring up your issues.It drains others and decreases their likelihood of finding you enjoyable. Try to be a positive person who sees the good in most situations.

9. Make fun of oneself

The folks who can laugh the hardest at themselves and their lives are usually the ones who are having the most fun. This lesson was the one I fully grasped until my senior year of high school.

At lunch one day in high school, a friend of mine cracked a joke about me.

I laughed because it was so amusing. He said something that I can't quite recall, but it wasn't what they were expecting from me.For the rest of high school and life, I was able to simply grin and laugh whenever someone made a joke with me.

Oddly enough, everyone ended up getting along with me for the most part despite the fact that I didn't really talk much.

The people that are most appreciated are the ones who can make fun of themselves, their mistakes, or just their personality in general.And don't you find that the most like able people are usually the ones who can laugh at themselves?.

10.Be fervent about the things you enjoy.

Even if people aren't always interested in the subjects you're passionate about, they could become so just by witnessing your enthusiasm. I have had many conversations with ardent movie fans.

Although I don't particularly enjoy watching movies, everytime I spoke to someone who did, my interest in the topic increased.

The same thing has always been true whenever I've talked about my love of music or my love of religious texts. I spoke with some people who weren't particularly religious.

The same thing has always been true whenever I've talked about my love of music or my love of religious texts. I spoke with some people who weren't particularly religious.

But as I started talking about it with all of my enthusiasm, they became even more interested in learning more.

As a result, you are having fun by sharing your enthusiasm for it, and others are having fun with you as a result of their increased interest in you.

It encourages conversation with you from others. Passion doesn't mean you have to convey this loud excitement about something. It's just showing how much you like what you're into.By the way, it also functions the other way around. Allow other people to share their true passions with you and decide to engage with them about it.

They'll be delighted to be able to express all their ideas and opinions about anything to someone who will genuinely listen.

11. Attempt to always have fun.

I think you can have fun with nearly anything. People prefer to like you because you know how to enjoy life when they realize that you know how to spend time in practically any circumstance.

What does it mean to always enjoy your time, you might be asking yourself right now. It's as easy as carrying out one of two strategies that have proven effective for me in my life and might do the same for you.

A, highlighting any aspects of your current situation that you think noteworthy.

It need not be significant or transformable; it might just be anything that attracts your attention. Perhaps something in a movie that you're viewing with someone strikes out to you.The other person may either see that thing on their own and find it intriguing, or they may respond to you, "Yeah, I noticed that too!" in which case a fleeting connection is made.

Because when another person notices the same thing they did, it usually makes everyone feel wonderful.

B, Discovering a method to enjoy yourself in whatever you're doing

There are those people in life with whom you can simply have a wonderful time doing whatever without having to do anything special. One of those folks can also be you.

Even in the most dull settings, you may pass the time by making jokes about your surroundings, being goofy, or just having nice conversation.

I've enjoyed watching folks pick up trash in a stadium, wait for a class to end, or do nothing at all.

12.

Try not to constantly speak the most amusing or fascinating thing.

I formerly believed that in order to engage someone in conversation, I had to say something amusing or fascinating. I would therefore attempt to be incredibly hilarious or to say something completely different was able to make people laugh most of the time just by speaking my views. Not even trying to be humorous here. You can thus just express what is on your mind and watch what occurs.

Normally, the situation would turn out to be really awkward. Everyone wants to be able to engage in conversation where others think them interesting or amusing.

Being sincere in your thoughts usually suffices when trying to say something that people find interesting. Really, how do you feel or think about something?.

13. Discover the world and its cultures.

The more information and life experiences you have, the easier it will be for you to relate to other people. I've heard before from someone that I can talk to you about anything.

It's because I've permitted myself to experiment with various aspects of life. Despite the fact that the subjects were ones I was always most interested in, I read and watched things out of curiosity.

I've traveled and experimented with new things. All of this translates into my ability to discuss a wide range of topics that other people may find interesting.

Even if I may not be as knowledgeable or experienced in those areas as they are, I can follow the discourse.

Having knowledge and experiences not only improves dialogue, but they also make you more intriguing as a person.

Because it's common for people to like knowing someone who has accomplished something unique.

14. Reduce your workload

Your best ally can be simplicity. Nobody appreciates being around folks who are excessively extravagant or problematic.

It may seem cool to be the loudest and wildest man in the room, but that attitude wears thin soon.

People can genuinely enjoy someone who is laid-back and doesn't constantly feel the need to speak.

I've discovered that a lot of people like being around me simply because I exude an uncommonly happy and relaxed atmosphere.

The majority of individuals talk too much and never seem to quit acting irrationally.

You'll be a welcome relief to someone, I assure you. Having said all of that, it's okay if you have a boisterous, colorful personality; just maybe dial it back occasionally.

15. Periodically send amusing or informative stories and videos.

I used to share things with a select people that I thought they may find amusing or intriguing. The majority of it was songs and singers because I love music.

People will remember you more favorably if they enjoy the material you send them

They think of you as having a sense of humor, being original, or simply having good taste in general.

Even though some of the material you send may not be well received, it still helps you succeed.

You're demonstrating your concern for that person. Whether someone calls them or merely sends them a small gift to brighten their day, people prefer to know that others are thinking of them.

Not only will you become more like able, but you'll also make people think of you as one of their favorite individuals.

16. Provide information that people may find useful.

I had a few pals who would give me job advertisements they came across when I was unemployed. I was quite grateful for it and began to like those people more as a result,

I would follow suit and email them job listings or any relevant advertisements that they would find useful. Perhaps you are aware of a problem or query that someone has recently been attempting to resolve.

Maybe they have something they want to get rid of, and you know someone who would be interested in it.

People will appreciate you a lot more if you help them with their difficulties or give them fresh ideas that might not have occurred to them before but could be helpful. This will turn someone into a friend very soon.

17. Be respectful

Today's society sometimes makes courtesy seem like a forgotten art. Some folks may be pleasantly surprised when you display it.For those who are following you, hold the door open. Don't speak during other people's conversations. If someone does anything nice for you, thank them.

Although it may all seem obvious, you'd be amazed at how many people don't think to take these simple steps.

18. Even when you disagree, show respect.

It seems more difficult than ever for individuals to respectfully differ in these polarized times.

Even when people disagree with what you say, if you truly demonstrate that you can accept their difference of opinion, they will still like you,

I've had chats with individuals that I strongly disagreed with.

However, I would just engage them in what they believed by asking questions rather than rebutting them and pointing out their errors.

There is always one larger perspective in their point of view that you may concur with.

Example: You state that you support tuition-free higher education. The opposing viewpoint affirms that earning a college education is possible,Well, getting an education is undoubtedly vital, and perhaps we can find the best solutions to make it more accessible to more people.

Simply having a civil conversation without insults or demeaning remarks will be very refreshing and endearing to the other person. Additionally, it will make people respect you.

19. Request favors infrequently

There's a school of thought that says you can increase your level of popularity by requesting favors from others.

It's mostly true, but I believe that people also genuinely appreciate people that don't ask for favors.

Consider this. If someone is aware of the fact that you don't constantly depend on them, they are aware of your genuine want to be their buddy.

In fact, aside from like you more, they'll likely offer to help you without even being asked.

Doing favors for people, in my opinion, will help you understand them better.If someone you know is struggling, see if there is anything you can do to help, or give them some suggestions.

They will value it even if the person replies, "Thanks, but I'll be alright," in such case. They'll be aware that you'll be there for them if they ever need assistance. That is how you win people over.

20. Give people food

Even though it may seem strange, individuals enjoy food. If you know how to cook or bake, or if you have the money to buy a meal, bring it the next time so the office may enjoy it.

It might be as straightforward as cookies. This is related to making someone associate you favorably in their thoughts.If they consume the food and genuinely enjoy it, you will score greatly on the like ability meter.

21. Avoid being a fraud

I've met across those folks in life who just seem absolutely false to me. I quickly recognized the BS in the words and didn't want anything to do with them.

The best way I can explain it is that the individual would be extremely amiable, overly polite, or just attempting to appear hilarious in a way that sounds too good to be true.

To be loved, you don't necessarily need to sound particularly kind or affable. Just be genuine and true to yourself.

22. Take it easy.

People will typically feel uptight around you if you are tense. Being in social situations might certainly be extremely nerve-wracking for some of you.

You sincerely hope to enjoy yourself and that other people will accept you for who you are. I am aware of how it feels.

I've occasionally struggled with anxiousness. But it will become simpler the more you put yourself in similar predicaments.However, as you gain the experience, make an effort to pay closer attention to how your body is feeling and make any necessary adjustments.Make sure your shoulders are relaxed, that your arms and legs are not crossed, and that you are just letting your body hang limp.

You aid others who may be equally anxious in feeling less tense by being relaxed. Every time you can convince someone to experience a bodily improvement, you score major brownie points with them.

23. Pay attention to what others tell you I've had folks react angrily when I bring up things they've mentioned in the past.It increases your likeability by demonstrating that you paid attention to them and that you care about them.

Remember the broad things like what they're most proud of or what their dreams are, as well as the minor things like that one sensation or circumstance they dislike.

24. Be Trustworthy

Do what you promise to do when you say you'll do it. Nowadays, people frequently break their promises. Even worse, they decide not to extend the courtesy of informing someone in advance that they must cancel.

I've tried my best to honor commitments I've made to be somewhere and do something with someone.i tried to always show up for the time I booked with someone, even when I wasn't feeling well.

I can assure you that it has increased my admiration and popularity among individuals I have encountered in real life.

Consider how much it can help you to stand out from the crowd if you are reliable in this day and age when it seems like so many others aren't.

That raises your likelihood of getting loved, becoming a close buddy, or perhaps even becoming far more.

25. Look after yourself

You may be wondering what having good self-care has to do with people loving you. You'll be astonished to learn that it can actually have a significant impact.

To begin with, if you take care of yourself physically, eat well, and get enough sleep, you're undoubtedly attractive.

And despite how self-centered it may sound, people do favor individuals who look nice over those who don't..

But something that matters considerably more than that is deeper still. You can't be your best self if you're not taking care of yourself as well as you should.

People like us more when we smile more, interact more, are more upbeat, and do all the other tiny things that have been described so far.

You typically don't feel good when you aren't adequately caring for yourself.

Your attitude is probably more negative, you're less involved, you're insecure, and you basically give off a feeling that makes people uncomfortable being around you.

If you really start looking after yourself, you can notice a significant difference in both how you and others connect with one another. They could begin to like you sincere.

Stand   to   win   forever.

4

How to *Really* Win Your Crush Back to YouAll the advice you'll need to seduce your crush.

1. Become more visible.

I am aware of how terrifying it might be, but sometimes you have to take the initiative. You can't expect your crush to be able to read your mind and realize that you're seriously crushing on them. Invite them over for a movie marathon, ask them out on a study date, or make an extra effort to speak with them. They might just reciprocate your feelings once they sense your attention, at which point everything will fall into place. Make things happen instead of waiting years for your crush to notice you.

2. . Use delicate hand motions.

The subtlest of expressions might catch your crush's eye. If you pass them in the hallway, compliment their attire or just smile and say hello. Keep things flirtatious over text after school. Asking them a question, sending them a funny joke or meme, or, if they play sports, congratulating them on a recent victory are all simple ways to do this.

3. Spend time with them, but don't indulge yourself too much!

Try to be around your crush as much as you can without coming off too strong. It might sound pretty obvious. Ask them to be your gym buddy, sit next to them at lunch, or even offer spending the weekend with. You two will get an opportunity to engage and connect during your one-on-one time, which may lead to a mutual attraction.

.

4. Listen!

Although it's enjoyable to chat about oneself, your crush definitely isn't interested in the time your Boyfriend accidentally fell in front of everyone at the mall (even though it was hilarious). Of course, you should inform others about yourself, but you also need to pay attention to your crush (not on your phone while they tell you about their siblings). Keep an open mind, participate, and pay attention to what they have to say. When you wish them luck on the test they casually mentioned a few days prior, your crush will be really grateful.

.

5. Find out the interests of your crush.

Find out what matters to someone if you want to "truly" get to know them. Ask your crush why they choose to work for Planned Parenthood if you see them volunteering there, or consider volunteering with them. "If you get someone to talk about something they like, it's going to put that person in a good mood, and you become part of the good vibes.

Nothing personally draws me to my crush more than witnessing them become excited about a subject or activity they are genuinely interested in. Inquiring about their priorities will not only help you get to know them better, but it will also provide you insight into their personality.

6. Establish eye contact.

Nothing is more embarrassing than a date where there is poor eye contact. Seriously! My recommendation? Keep eye contact with the person you like if you are seated across from them at the table and throughout the entire talk. While they are stuffing food into their mouths, you don't have to stare at them, but you should keep your head up and glance up whenever you are speaking, looking about the room, or using your phone. You'll appear uninterested or give your crush the impression that you'd rather be somewhere else if you glance away from them. Nobody desires that! Additionally, maintaining eye contact can make you seem more certain, which will only increase your attractiveness to them.

7. Get your crush a warm beverage.

Okay, to be honest, I've never done this, but when someone is holding a warm beverage, they are more likely to perceive the person they are speaking with—that is, YOU—as having a personality they like. Additionally, science is always right, so why not give it a shot?

8. . Don't hesitate to express your emotions.

I know that it seems "cool" to play the game, and I've definitely had my fair share of occasions where playing the game has been useful to helping me get closer to my infatuation. But, to be honest, none of my four previous relationships had started out after I played the field. Instead, after one of us was open about our feelings for the other, they developed into a genuine partnership. I understand that doing something requires courage, but if I can do it FOUR times in my life (and have never looked back), you can too.

9. Seriously, don't trick people.

One (or both) of you could get hurt, and it is not worth anyone's attention. You might only lose this individual by failing to respond for several hours or even days, making them constantly envious, or simply ignoring them. Mind games significantly worsen the situation, and getting through a crowd is already challenging enough! Being open and honest about your emotions is crucial, especially with yourself.

10. Be authentic!

One of the worst flirting blunders, in my opinion, is to pretend to be someone you're not in real life. The truth is that if you're trying to be someone else that you believe your crush will enjoy, you'll be in trouble if they start to like that person instead of you since it's not you! Seriously. Be yourself because you want your crush to like YOU, not a version of you, from the moment you start hanging out with them until you "eventually maybe become official."

11.Display your unique sense of style.

When getting to know someone, it's crucial to be authentic, and this extends to your clothing choices as well. Do not simply put on an outfit because you believe it will appeal to them or because it is popular. Dress to impress! If you enjoy wearing band t-shirts, your personal style can even spark a conversation

12. In their presence, put down your phone!

Put down your phone when you're with your crush, it should go without saying. Your time is important with them, and you're definitely going to text your crush everything later anyway. Therefore, group chats and YouTube cosmetics tutorials may wait. Pay attention to your crush. Pose questions to them. Describe yourself, your favorite books, and your aspirations to them. Avoid being sidetracked. Give them your undivided attention at all times. After all, they are your crush. They are due it

13. Talk about them with your pals.

This will help you put your "crush problem" into perspective. Inform your closest friends about your conversations and their texts, and then reexamine the situation. Since it can be difficult to see things objectively when you have a crush on someone, friends can be a great resource for helping you put the issue in perspective. They might like you more than you think. Or perhaps you discover that you don't like them as much as you thought when you first saw them.

14. Don't discuss your previous crushes.

irrespective of what occurs. Never discuss past relationships with ex-boyfriends, crushes, flings, dates, or breakups with your new crush. How would you feel if your crush opened up to you about their previous relationships? The fastest method to "friend-zone" someone in your life is to do that as well. Besides, group conversations are for discussing previous romances!

15. Never press for a conversation.

While being honest and upfront with your crush is great, you don't want to disclose too much or push them too much. There is no use in hurrying through the getting to know you stage because it is one of the most exhilarating in any new relationship. Yes, word vomit can happen, but try to let some topics naturally come up in discussion.

16. Tell them what you like about them.

Be as sincere as you can about this. Do they frequently sit next to you in math class because of the way they enter the room? Is it the contributions they make in English class? a game they're good at? their hair's natural fall? What is it about them that keeps running through your mind? What distinguishes them? Sometimes it's more difficult to identify than you think, but once you do, don't be hesitant to let them know what it is. Everyone enjoys receiving compliments, and I'm sure your crush would feel incredibly proud to have one from someone as amazing as you.

17. Never lose sight of your own value.

You are not any less emotionally resilient just because you are completely consumed by your crush. Before your first date and, ideally, as you go toward a closer relationship with your crush, keep this in mind. You have so many positive qualities. How could someone not swoon over you?

You've got it now. go with assurance. Be confident. Put your phone away and ask your crush what they have planned for the weekend. You can accomplish it if I can!.

5

What makes me want to be someone else?

I What makes me want to be someone else? come to a point in their lives where they will look in the mirror and feel unhappy and disillusioned with who they see. They see someone who hasn't been cared for the way they should have been, the way they deserve, and this makes them unhappy with themselves and makes them wish they didn't have to live their life as this person they have become.

They observe a person who requires love and care. They observe a non-respected individual. They observe a person who hasn't received anything so essential as love and sympathy. The worst aspect of it all is that the person who failed to offer and show love to this person they no longer wished to be—the one who was negligent, disrespectful, and abandoned—was their own self..

They are aware that they are capable of giving themselves considerably better care and attention. They are aware that they had every possibility to succeed and that they were able to do it all. They are aware of the full extent of the potential they had in their control and the portion of it they just wasted.

They may regret the life they chose to live and wish they had chosen a different path after seeing the consequences of all their missed opportunities and unrealized potential, as well as realizing how awful their current situation is in comparison to what they know it could have been.

Have I already made you all cry and feel down? Do you now wish that you hadn't chosen to read more instead of desiring to be someone else? But don't give up on me just yet. I can give you some hope, though. And you might not like the little bit of illumination I can offer to this gloomy realm of your sadness. You might not feel any happier, but pleasing you was never my goal. The only thing I wanted to convey with this was how much hurt you may suffer from carelessness, contempt, and abandonment.

Do these still hold true? Absolutely.

You will soon find yourself in a pretty terrible state if you don't take care of yourself and if you don't learn how to offer and show love to yourself. All of it was made possible by and due to you, including the person you don't want to be and the life you're unhappy and disappointed with. You have made every decision that has brought you one step closer to the person you don't want to be. You are what and who you are because of yourself. Everything about who you are, both the things you love and the things you despise, are products of your own decisions.

Let's now look for a glimmer of hope in all of that. You can develop self-love and appreciation. You can begin taking better care of yourself than you have. You have the power to change into anyone you choose to be. You can make your life better than it is right now. You can conduct yourself with some respect and civility. You can take better care of yourself and be more considerate of yourself. As long as you begin the work, you may actually enjoy your life and feel pleased with who you are. Your effort must be more remarkable the more exceptional you want to be.

A person who works hard to live a meaningful and satisfying life is someone who is worth being. It may sound sweet and simple to love and take care of oneself, but I can assure you that it is not. If it had been, you wouldn't ever want to want to be anyone else. If self-love and self-care were ever simple, you wouldn't have chosen to neglect yourself so frequently that it became ingrained in your behavior.

Break the habit of not treating yourself with the respect you deserve. Put more effort into selecting the best course of action for yourself. Don't just sit about wishing you were someone you're not.

Don't waste time wishing away your life. Never be slack. Increase the amount of time and effort you put into becoming the person you want to be.

The other half of who you can be is still hidden from you. You never know how amazing you might be or how much you might love being precisely who you are.

Due to the fact that you are not happy with who you are. You feel jealous of others because of the things they possess. That shouldn't be how you feel. Love yourself; recognize that each person is unique. Someone may be envious of you because you possess a quality they don't have. Accept your shortcomings and love yourself. Never forget that nobody is flawless. They might be excellent in all aspects of life, yet you share something with them that they don't. Just be who you are.

6

What You Can Do to Stop Thinking About the Life You Could Be Living.

You will never have enough if you focus on what you don't have.

I've frequently made comparisons to other people and thought that their lives were better than mine.

I was raised with a mother who frequently remarked, "So and so must really be happy! Check them out! They are adept at living life.

She often wished her life had been different because she had eight children to raise after becoming a widower at the age of forty. These ideas and words stuck with me in some way.

Despite being a professor and researcher who has written books, I have frequently felt inadequate.

Despite everything I've done and accomplished in my life, I frequently catch myself believing that other people have it better than I do (despite all the webinars, self-development books, self-improvement mp3 and meditations I have done).

I contrast myself with those who, in some way, "seem" to have a more enjoyable life. I used to believe that other scholars were constantly "creating" more than I was at the beginning of my career.

The idea that I might be experiencing multiple lives is another example of this way of thinking.

Let me explain: Sometimes we get trapped thinking that the past, or what we prefer to call our "missed opportunities," is better than the present.

We might think along these lines:

"I'd be living my dreams if I had done such and such."

I might be doing something else in another place instead of leading this exciting life.

I'd be so content if I had..."

The issue is in this area.

Opportunities are lost when we are not in the present moment.

If we are not attentive of our present, about the now here, we are nowhere when we live in the now while regretting the past and dreaming of a future that might never arrive.

No one can be content if they are not in the moment.

I feel awful when I remain in that mindset. I experience victimization and a sense of inadequacy or failure. All falsehoods.
These enormous lies originate in our anxieties, egos, and shadows. This occurs as a result of our identification with ideas of what we may have done or ought to be doing. The alternative is to practice mindfulness.

I've come to the realization that I must learn to distinguish between my love voice and my ego. What sensations do each of these cause in my body? Here are my opinions about it:

Inner voice:

If you were somewhere else, it would be so much better. Life is much better on the other side. You may be content living somewhere, but you're confined to this place. You missed the chance to experience this life. You stumbled.
These ideas make me uneasy, afraid, tense, and twitchy.

0
    Love says:

Your life is wonderful and you have so many possibilities and opportunities, right here and right now. You are wonderful and you are loved. Open your eyes to the doors of opportunity near you, to the beauty that you already create right here and right now. All is well.

These thoughts bring peace and calm to my body and heart.

, "The ego looks for what to criticize. This always involves comparing with the past. But love looks upon the world peacefully and accepts. The ego searches for short comings and weaknesses. Love watches for any sign of strength. It sees how far each one has come, and not how far he has to go."
    Love claims
    Your life is amazing, and you have a ton of options and chances available to you right now. You are adored and wonderful. Open your eyes to the doors of opportunity that are right in front of you and to the beauty that you are already producing right now. It's all good.
    My body and heart feel at ease and at ease thinking about these things.

The ego searches for things to criticize. This always includes looking backward in time. But love accepts and has a serene perspective on the world. The ego looks for flaws and areas of weakness. Love is alert for any indication of fortitude. It looks at each person's progress rather than how far they still have to go.

So how do we escape this rut? How can we live our lives while being more mindful of who we are? This list was created by me for better assistance, and it might just do the trick.

1. Breathe first.
    With each breath, we connect with our higher selves and the present moment. Take a deep breath if you catch yourself comparing or thinking about the past.

2. Play some music.

Life without music would be a mistake, . Turn up your favorite song when you start to feel bad about yourself. Since music is the language of love, you'll soon start singing along, getting in the zone, and enjoying the moment.

3. Recite a mantra.

I've discovered that mantras can be incredibly effective tools for empowerment and mindfulness. "I Am the Light" is the one I enjoy the best. I have the Light within.

4.

Proclaim affirmations.

Every morning before I get up, I repeat the ones I've created or copied that speak to me.

I accept everything as it is, tell yourself whenever you catch yourself thinking back on the past. It's all good. I have faith in divine order. I value everything I have and everything I am.

Claim these words and really feel it as you say them.

5. Pose in some yoga.

Get your energy moving with some yoga poses, such as the child stance, downward dog, or the tree pose, if you feel stuck. If yoga is new to you, you might want to begin with some simple stretches while breathing in time with the motions.

6. Be in awe of the natural world.

In order to nourish us, nature is here. Take a step back and observe the environment around you if you are feeling empty or lost in your self-deprecating thoughts about yourself and your life. When birds visit my house's backyard to dine, I enjoy watching them. Their freedom inspires me to remember that, if I so choose, I can also be free.

7. Be appreciative of all that you have and are.

Gratitude is effective because it helps us focus on all the positive things in our lives rather than always comparing ourselves to others and their possessions. In fact, saying, "Thank you for everything. No complaints from me.

8. Make one small change today to lead the life you want (instead of dwelling on the life you could have had).

What can you do today to actively create the world you envision? that's what you should be asking yourself.

9. Enjoin the moment!

Being mindful is paying attention to all the little details that make life interesting. It entails scheduling leisure time as well. It could be taking a walk, writing in your diary, singing along to your favorite music, or simply enjoying your favorite dish.

Enjoy your present location and this wonderful world. The most essential thing is to embrace who you are right now, just as you are!

I still have times when I wish I had a different life, but I use those times to learn to appreciate the present and practice living in the now. I'm getting better at viewing these instances as brief cues to present-day living.

Just put your efforts to become who you want to be.

7

Nine techniques to help you stop ruminating on the bad.

Work, your relationship, or some great stuff are causing you anxiety. Even while you may believe that your efforts to fix problems are being useful if you are continuously thinking about the past and what you might have done better, obsessively concentrating on difficulties from the past might be detrimental rather than beneficial.

Rumination sounds like it might be a problem for you if you have a hard time letting go and feel the need to constantly try to sort through the past.

What is ruminating?

Ruminating is when someone thinks excessively or becomes fixated on a problem or event in their life. Some people are more likely to engage in rumination than others, particularly if they have an anxious personality. Rumination is the act of dwelling on past events that cannot be changed.

Examples include rehashing terrible past experiences in your head, rehearsing dialogues, concentrating on injuries or injustices, or asking seemingly intractable questions like "why me?" The main feature of all cases of rumination is that the individual becomes stuck on a single subject, experience, or feeling.

People who ruminate overthink or obsess on things or occurrences in their lives.

Rumination can take two forms. If you discover that reflecting on the past and evaluating various situations might provide you with answers and closure, the outcome can be positive. However, if you find yourself

35

going over and over the same problem without getting anywhere, your private and public life may suffer, as well as your mental health.

Rumination's negative effects

It is critical to learn to let go of bad thoughts and feelings without allowing them to control your life.

'Rumination can have a bad impact on your mental health,'. 'It is linked to anxiety disorders and sadness, and it can even be a cause of these problems.'

If you believe you are suffering from rumination, try the following expert advice to help you calm the demons:

1. Is it really worth it?

If you find yourself obsessed on a particular scenario, consider whether the dwelling is genuinely worth your time.

'Ask yourself if revisiting a particular incident will help you accept it, learn from it, and achieve closure,'. 'If the answer is no, you should make a concerted effort to put the subject aside and move on.

2. . Make time to think.

Niggling concerns frequently linger in the back of your mind, always present but never given your complete focus. By devoting time to whatever is upsetting you, you will be able to address the issue once and for all.

Write down your thoughts on a piece of paper and set aside time during the day to reflect on them.

Whenever you begin to dwell, jot the notion down on a piece of paper and set aside time during the day to think about it, ideally a few hours later,'. 'This will offer you some space from the dwelling, which means it won't annoy you as much in a few hours, as well as helping you to focus on other, more important things during the day.'

3. Consider the worst-case scenario.

If you find yourself obsessing on anything that happened, consider the worst-case situation and how you would handle it.

'It may sound like a bad idea, but having a feasible answer available will leave you feeling calmer and less stressed, as well as pleasantly surprising you if things come out better than planned, which is often the case.

4. Identify your source of anxiety.

There may be a pattern in your concerns, which means you can assist in identifying potential causes and implementing preventative measures.

Rumination will come after a trigger for many of us, therefore it is crucial to define what it is,' 'For example, if you have to deliver a presentation at work and the last one didn't go as planned, you may experience rumination and worry.

'Once you've identified this trigger, set aside some time to review your previous mistakes and make sure you don't repeat them, which will remove the stimulus of rumination.'

8

How To Stop Preferring A Person You Can't Date

Are you considering someone you can't be with all the time? It's not necessary to completely let go of someone once you realize you should stop liking them, but you can do it eventually. Make room for yourself and speak up for what you need. This is a time to find yourself and maintain your own identity while moving forward.

1.It's acceptable

Maintain a relationship with this person that is acceptable for the situation. This implies that if you like your boss, make sure you maintain a professional and respectful tone in all of your dealings. If you find yourself wondering "Why am I suddenly drawn to my female friend?" but you know she doesn't feel the same way about you, resolve to merely be her friend or even reconsider whether you can have her in your life. If you find yourself fantasizing about someone, it is impossible to quit like them. Don't engage in interactions that are inappropriate for your relationship; otherwise, you'll meet someone else. Eventually, your feelings should start to fade.

2. Take a break.

You may have made an effort to maintain a professional or friendly relationship with your crush, but you still find it infuriating that you can't be together. You can't keep your cool amongst them since they're constantly on your mind. It can be wise to keep your distance for a while or to cut off all contact. Of course, that isn't always possible at work, but it can be useful to find a way to keep your distance till your emotions pass.

3. Set limitations.

Setting limits is essential. Perhaps you're falling for a close friend who always wants to be with you but is unaware of your feelings for them. Setting boundaries in such a circumstance may be wise. For whatever reason, you are unable to express how much you want this person in your life. You can limit the amount of time you spend together. There is a potential that you can be friends even if you can express how you feel to them and they don't feel the same way. Each of you should agree to refrain from flirting or saying things that could be interpreted differently in this situation

4. Set limitations.

Setting limits is essential. Perhaps you're falling for a close friend who always wants to be with you but is unaware of your feelings for them. Setting boundaries in such a circumstance may be wise. For whatever reason, you are unable to express how much you want this person in your life. You can limit the amount of time you spend together. There is a potential that you can be friends even if you can express how you feel to them and they don't feel the same way. Each of you should agree to refrain from flirting or saying things that could be interpreted differently in this situation

5. Let someone know how you are feeling.

You can stop obsessing and start feeling more normal by talking to someone about how you are feeling. Avoid talking to those who know the person you admire or spreading rumors! Talk to someone outside of that circle or someone you trust so that you don't cause any drama or rumors

6, Managing Obtrusive Thoughts

Are you experiencing uncontrollable thoughts and memories? Maybe it's a nagging thought that won't go away no matter how hard you try to shut it out. Everyone has intrusive thoughts occasionally, and they can do so during this process. They could feel more persistent in your thoughts since you find it difficult to resist the want to like them and push them out of your head. "Intrusive thoughts" are these undesired and persistent ideas. It's normal to occasionally have intrusive ideas, and it can be difficult to try to push these "bad thoughts" away. Stay away from situations that can set them off, such frequently checking their social media accounts or watching love movies. Make a plan to participate in alternative, less triggering actions whenever there is a chance that a scenario can "trigger" intrusive thoughts. Everyone has intrusive ideas occasionally, and since they can occur in a number of contexts, you should simply let them to pass through your mind the next time they do.

7.Be practical

You don't need to be rescued, and this person is not a prince or princess in disguise. People who have difficulties letting go of someone they liked may be extending the relationship in their imaginations through remembering and fantasizing. Fantasy makes it difficult to back away or let go, as it's addictive and produces a "rush." The process is driven by your refusal to accept that you are enmeshed in a fiction. Let go of any fantasies you may have about being with the individual to begin with. Before spending time with someone, you truly can't understand what it's like. It can turn out to be quite different from what you anticipated—and not in a good way.

8 .Additional Options

To cease liking someone, it makes sense to leave and accept the circumstance. You might have to feel regret for what you believed might have been. You might have feelings of loss for the person you liked while going through this grieving process. Processing your feelings with them is not necessary for successfully stepping away from them because it is likely to strengthen the bond. You can do a few things to stop thinking about these things.

Journaling is one remedy. Write the person a letter in your journal explaining why you can't stand them any longer. The message should make it clear why you don't think the relationship can work and state a hard limit you'll uphold moving forward. You can also change your thought process. Turn your attention away from this person whenever you find yourself doing so. Instead of thinking about someone outside of your relationship, think about your existing partner. In professional studies, this has produced excellent outcomes.

Sometimes the pressure of liking someone you can't date becomes too much. Try some soothing exercises like yoga or meditation if this describes you. Anything that helps you unwind and maintain your sense of reality will work.

Why Better Help Can Be of Use

Even if it seems like you've tried everything with no luck, there are still other things you can try. As you handle powerful feelings for someone and attempt to move forward in your life, seeking knowledgeable professional assistance may be the wise course of action.

Make a step.

9

18 Ways to Stop Trying to Please Everyone

You could feel as though you have no free time if you engage in people-pleasing behavior. you may reclaim your life with a few helpful hints.

maybe you've heard that people adore you because they know you'll go above and beyond to fulfill their needs.However, there is a downside: Recently, you have accepted every request made of you, even when you don't want to.

Or perhaps you feel bad every time you have to refuse anything. Regardless of the situation, the risk of trying to please everyone is that it may leave you feeling emotionally spent, anxious, and burned out.

Do I try to please everyone?
Numerous other characteristics are linked to people-pleasing behavior. Also, people-pleasers might:

Be accommodative, avoid conflict, struggle to say no, feel overwhelmed or agitated, and display passive aggression.
being prone to anger
be quick to assign blame and struggle to uphold their convictions

How to stop being a people pleaser
It's not always simple to put an end to people-pleasing conduct. it can be challenging to disagree with people since doing so increases cognitive dissonance, a mismatch between your values and the behavior you desire to pursue.

The following advice could be helpful:

*. Recognize that you are free to choose.

Despite the fact that it could seem like an instinctual response, you do have a choice. Often, the first step toward transformation is awareness.

*. Choose your priorities.

Saying no to anything that doesn't support your life goals gets simpler once you have figured out what your priorities are and the kinds of people you want to spend time with.

*. Establish limits.

It could be beneficial to see boundaries as the external manifestation of self-love.

Once you've decided what you're willing to do, gently express your needs to others.

Don't be shocked if some of your connections fade away and your relationships start to shift. It might be simpler to hold the line if you are aware of this beforehand.

"Because you're so accustomed to taking care of other people and their feelings, speaking your actual feelings out loud will initially be frightening. Your efforts to live an authentic life will be praised by those who love and support you,

Most likely, those who react defensively or angrily are those who gain from your people-pleasing lifestyle and feel threatened by your newfound freedom.

Pruden continues, "It could be time to assess and adjust your support system.

* Set a deadline.

Tell the caller you're on your way out the door when you pick up the phone. Tell someone your arrival time requirement when you schedule a date.

Time blocking not only increases productivity but also gives you the option to abruptly stop helping someone. Consider it as avoiding the adage "give an inch, take a mile."

* Think about whether you're being misled.

Pay attention to anyone in your life who flatters you excessively to get you to do something. It may be presented as a complement when in reality it's an attempt to get someone else to do something they don't want to. You might hear manipulators say, "I would love to take on that assignment, but you're just so much more knowledgeable about this subject than I am. You'll perform much better.

* Invent a mantra.

A motivational phrase written down somewhere you'll see it frequently, such on your phone's backdrop or the bathroom mirror, can serve as a tiny pep talk throughout the day.

Try repeating the mantra, "I'm permitted to say no."

A whole sentence is "No."

For me, a "no" to them is a "yes."

Not my monkeys, not my circus.

I'm not required to defend myself to anyone.

My time and my energy belong to me.

*Saying "no" firmly

Even though you know you're not interested, it may be tempting as a people-pleaser to respond to an invitation with "maybe" or "I don't know."

Cut yourself some slack instead by declining in a tactful yet respectful manner. Try these if telling someone no outright sounds too harsh:

Saying, "I won't be able to make it," might work.

I'm sorry, I'm at capacity.

I'll have to decline taking on that task.

Although I'm honored, someone else can devote the time that is due.

Thank you for thinking about me even though I have plans that day.

* Request time

"start delaying the yes to practice saying no

Say something like: Let me think about that.

Let me check my calendar when I go home as I don't have it with me right now.

I should ask my [partner] because I'm unsure if we have any plans for that weekend.

* Sit uncomfortable

People-pleasing is a strategy used by certain people to lessen the severe discomfort associated with rejection, condemnation, desertion, or feeling less-than-ideal. However, if you can learn to sit with those emotions, they might have less influence on your behavior.

* Don't list a bunch of justifications

More people can convince you to change your mind about your choices the more information you provide, especially if they have weak boundaries. Try to be as general and on time with your no's.

a friendly reminder (to yourself)

After you deny a request, one tip to prevent rambling, offering excuses, or sounding uncertain is to think:

No comma, please. Sentence concluded.

* small at first

It could be beneficial for you to role-play with a friend, relative, or therapist. Ask them questions that you may refuse to answer. Play around with various body language, tones, and phrases.

* Practice "continuous improvement" by consecutive approximation. Big or minor changes don't matter as long as you're heading in the right way.

Be optimistic. You won't be able to completely modify your script overnight, but you can give your mental health some breathing room by making little adjustments.

*Don't apologize if you weren't at fault.
It could be tempting to apologize if you recommend a restaurant and your colleague's order is incorrect because you chose the place, after all.

There is an alternative.

Try saying: "I'm sorry that occurred to you," if it was truly not your fault.

* Include uplifting self-talk.
Inform your inner child of your success in undoing your previous lessons. Self-affirming phrases should be used.

Saying "My voice matters" might help.
I'm lovable just for 'being,' not for what I do.

* Celebrate your advancement.
It takes effort to get over people-pleasing. Many others wouldn't be willing to put in the effort and endure the discomfort, but you are.

Spend some time enjoying your successes.

* Maintain a confidence file.
Make a list on your phone of all the ways you're overcoming your people-pleasing tendencies. Refer to it whenever you need a confidence boost.

* Keep in mind that you can't please everyone all the time.
There will always be someone who doesn't like what you do. You can't convert everyone. At the end of the day, your opinion of yourself is more important than anyone else.

*Seek out expert assistance

"EMDR, or 'Eye movement Desensitization and Reprocessing,' will help someone process trauma memories that have led to the need for people-pleasing and lessen the dread, anxiety, and guilt that comes with asking for help or refusing someone."

Kick it .